SNOW SISTERS!

Kerri Kokias ✦ Teagan White

Alfred A. Knopf   New York

Snow!

Snow.

Coat. Scarf. Hat.
Mittens. Boots.

Cocoa. Blankets. Books.

Throwing. Building.

Baking. Making.

Tracking. Hiding.

Playing. Spotting.

Cold. Wet. Brrr.

Coat. Scarf. Hat.
Mittens. Boots.

Bye.

Bye.

Boots. Mittens. Hat.
Scarf. Coat.

Brrr. Wet. Cold. DISCARD

Spotting. Playing.

Hiding. Tracking.

Making. Baking.

Building. Throwing.

Books. Blankets. Cocoa.

Boots. Mittens. Hat.
Scarf. Coat.

Snow.

Snow!

Snow sisters!

To my family: May we always see the ways we're connected, even when we're apart. —K.K.

THIS IS A BORZOI BOOK PUBLISHED BY ALFRED A. KNOPF

Text copyright © 2018 by Kerri Kokias

Jacket art and interior illustrations copyright © 2018 by Teagan White

All rights reserved. Published in the United States by Alfred A. Knopf, an imprint of

Random House Children's Books, a division of Penguin Random House LLC, New York.

Knopf, Borzoi Books, and the colophon are registered trademarks of Penguin Random House LLC.

Visit us on the Web! randomhousekids.com

Educators and librarians, for a variety of teaching tools, visit us at RHTeachersLibrarians.com

Library of Congress Cataloging-in-Publication Data is available upon request.

ISBN 978-1-101-93883-6 (trade) — ISBN 978-1-101-93884-3 (lib. bdg.) — ISBN 978-1-101-93885-0 (ebook)

The illustrations in this book were created using gouache and watercolor.

MANUFACTURED IN CHINA

January 2018

10 9 8 7 6 5 4 3 2 1

First Edition